I like the
SNOW

written by Sarah Nelson • illustrated by Rachel Oldfield

Barefoot Books
step inside a story

I like the snow –

crunching underneath my toes,
icy kisses on my nose,
on my eyelids, chin and cheeks.
This is how the snow speaks.

I like the snow –

flower-flurries, floating, whirling,
stars and diamonds, twinkling, twirling.

Every snowflake is unique.

(I catch them on
my tongue to eat.)

I like making angels
flap and fly

and trudging tracks
that spell out "HI."

I like tunnelling and rolling!

I like climbing, sliding, throwing!

I like whooshing gusts
of cold, cold snow

and walls of white that blow and blow —

whistling windows, cocoa, pillows,

heaps of snow that wrap and billow.

I like drifting into winter dreams

and waking up to snow that gleams.

Glossy, golden, flashy, frozen,
bright and light –

I like the snow.

Questions for a Snowy Day

What is snow?

Snowflakes are clusters of tiny ice crystals. High in the clouds, the air is sometimes so cold that water (in the form of an invisible gas) freezes into ice crystals. When these crystals grow too heavy for the air to hold, they flutter from the clouds as snow.

Why are snowflakes so beautiful?

Snow freezes in complicated shapes. The shapes, called ice crystals, have six branches or six sides. Ice crystals, especially those that form in very cold skies, can look like stars, flowers, jewels or elegant glass plates. No two are exactly the same. Ice crystals that form in warmer skies are often six-sided sticks, tubes or even tiny, icy needles.

Why is snow white?

Snowflakes are not actually white — they are clear, like glass. But light bounces in many directions from all the tiny details on a snowflake. This makes snow look sparkly and white. Sunlight on snow can be so bright and white that some people wear sunglasses to protect their eyes.

How does snow help us?

In winter, snow acts as a blanket of insulation protecting tree roots and hibernating animals from extreme cold. When snow melts, fresh water fills rivers and lakes and seeps into our gardens, farm fields and our sources of drinking water. Water that was once snow may eventually be used for bathing, washing clothes or cooking food. Thank you, snow!

Enjoy more weather fun with *I Like the Rain*, *I Like the Sun* and *I Like the Wind*.

For Anne and her snow bunnies — S. N.

For my goddaughter Molly with love — R. O.

Barefoot Books
23 Bradford Street, 2nd Floor
Concord, MA 01742

Barefoot Books
29/30 Fitzroy Square
London, W1T 6LQ

Printed in China
This book was typeset in Century Gothic, Cut-Out,
Dear St. Nick and Mr Lucky
The illustrations were prepared in acrylics

Graphic design by Elizabeth Jayasekera, Barefoot Books
Edited and art directed by Kate DePalma, Barefoot Books
Reproduction by Bright Arts, Hong Kong

Hardback ISBN 978-1-64686-096-8   •   E-book ISBN 978-1-64686-018-0

British Cataloguing-in-Publication Data:
a catalogue record for this book is available from the British Library

Library of Congress Cataloging-in-Publication Data
is available under LCCN 2020009325

3 5 7 9 8 6 4

Barefoot Books
step inside a story

At Barefoot Books, we celebrate art and story that opens the hearts
and minds of children from all walks of life, focusing on themes that
encourage independence of spirit, enthusiasm for learning and respect
for the world's diversity. The welfare of our children is dependent on
the welfare of the planet, so we source paper from sustainably managed
forests and constantly strive to reduce our environmental impact.
Playful, beautiful and created to last a lifetime, our products combine
the best of the present with the best of the past to educate our
children as the caretakers of tomorrow.

www.barefootbooks.com

Sarah Nelson

lives with her husband in Minnesota, USA, where she loves making tracks in freshly fallen snow. Sarah is also a teacher and the author of several books for young children, including *Frogness*. Learn more about Sarah and her books at sarahnelsonbooks.com.

Rachel Oldfield

lives with her husband, three sons and three cats in England, where she teaches illustration at the University of Gloucestershire. She can also be found taking her horse Billy for walks along the country lanes. In addition to the I Like the Weather series, Rachel has illustrated *Up, Up, Up!* and *Outdoor Opposites* for Barefoot Books.